Geronimo Stilton

THE **JOURNEY THROUGH TIME**

PYRAMID PUZZLE

D0169563

Scholastic Inc.

ISBN 978-0-545-61128-2

Based on an original idea by Elisabetta Dami.

www.geronimostilton.com

Published by Scholastic Inc., 557 Broadway, New York, NY 10012. SCHOLASTIC and associated logos are trademarks and/or registered trademarks of Scholastic Inc.

Stilton is the name of a famous English cheese. It is a registered trademark of the Stilton Cheese Makers' Association. For more information, go to www.stiltoncheese.com.

Text by Geronimo Stilton
Original title *Viaggio nel tempo*
Cover by Silvia Bigolin (pencils and inks) and Christian Aliprandi (color)
Illustrations concept by Lorenzo Chiavini, Blasco Pisapia, Roberto Ronchi, and Valeria Turati
Illustrations production by Silvia Bigolin, Danilo Barozzi, Valeria Brambilla, Giuseppe Guindani (pencils and inks), Christian Aliprandi (color), and Francesco Barbieri
Graphics by Merenguita Gingermousee, Zeppola Zap, and Yuko Egusa with Chiara Cebraro and Studio Editoriale Littera

Special thanks to AnnMarie Anderson
Translated by Lidia Tramontozzi
Interior design by Kay Petronio

12 11 10 9 8 7 6 5 4 3   14 15 16 17 18 19/0

Printed in U.S.A.   40

This edition first printing, January 2014

TRAVELERS ON
THE JOURNEY THROUGH TIME

Dear rodent friends,
My name is Stilton, *Geronimo Stilton*. I am the editor and publisher of *The Rodent's Gazette*, the most famous newspaper on Mouse Island. I'm about to tell you the story of one of my most amazing adventures. Let me introduce you to the other mice you will meet. . . .

THEA STILTON

My sister, Thea, is a special correspondent for *The Rodent's Gazette*. She is very athletic and one of the most stubborn and determined mice I have ever met!

BENJAMIN

My nephew Benjamin is the sweetest and most affectionate little mouselet in the whole world.

TRAP

My cousin Trap is an incredible prankster. His favorite pastime is playing jokes on me.

PROFESSOR PAWS VON VOLT

Professor von Volt is a genius inventor who has dedicated his life to making amazing new discoveries. This time, he built a time machine!

New Mouse City, Present Day

Dear mouse friends,

The story you are about to read may be hard to believe, but it is true — every last word of it! I give you my rodent's word! When I learned that my friend Professor Paws von Volt had invented a **time machine**, I couldn't believe it. But then my family and I traveled to prehistoric times with the professor, where we saw real live **dinosaurs**!

This is my family with Professor von Volt

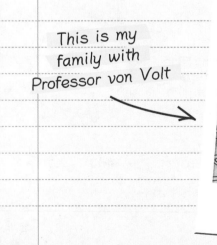

Just before our departure

While we were visiting prehistoric times, we collected rock and plant **specimens** and researched the real reason dinosaurs became **extinct**. I

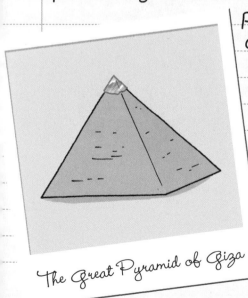

Mousenapped by a dinosaur!

even took a ride in the claws of a Rhamphorhynchus! That was an experience I will never forget.

After our successful journey through prehistory, Thea, Trap, Benjamin, the professor, and I decided to go on another **adventure**. This time, we headed to ancient Egypt, where we hoped to discover how the amazing Great Pyramid of Giza was built!

The Great Pyramid of Giza

My family and I climbed into the time machine, the Mouse Mover 3000. Professor von Volt set the Chronometer to take us to ancient Egypt. Then he pressed the departure button. The little ship began to vibrate and fill with a BLUE MIST. . . . .

The professor's time machine is shaped like a giant slice of cheese!

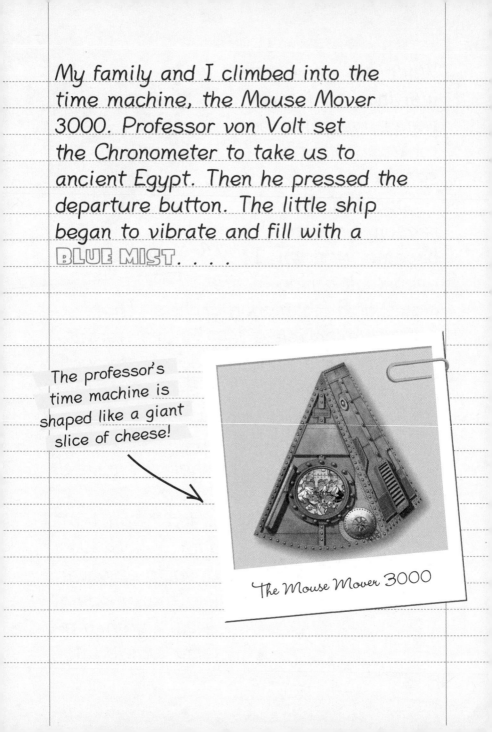

The Mouse Mover 3000

EGYPT

LIFE IN ANCIENT EGYPT

In 3000 BC, it is believed that the legendary **King Menes** unified the tribes of Upper and Lower Egypt and began the first of the thirty Egyptian dynasties. This civilization created one of the first forms of writing and the first solar calendar. The ancient Egyptians also made great advances in sculpture, poetry, architecture, mathematics, geometry, and medicine.

The Egyptians depended on the **Nile River** as a source of drinking water and to help them grow crops. The river's periodic floods left the ground rich with **mud** and **lime**, making the soil around the river very fertile.

After every flood, the field's boundaries were redrawn.

A BRIEF HISTORY OF PAPYRUS

PAPYRUS WAS ONE OF THE EARLIEST FORMS OF PAPER. THE PAPYRUS PLANT WAS COMMON AROUND THE NILE RIVER IN ANCIENT EGYPT, AND THE EGYPTIANS USED IT TO CREATE A THICK, PAPERLIKE WRITING MATERIAL. THEY ALSO USED THE PLANT IN THE CONSTRUCTION OF BOATS, MATTRESSES, MATS, ROPES, SANDALS, AND BASKETS.

Egyptian engineers used this tool — a plumb bob — in astronomy, navigation, surveying, and building.

The shaduf was one tool used by the Egyptians to water their crops.

In the Shadow of the Sphinx

I plugged my ears, gritted my teeth, and closed my eyes.

Bang! The **MOUSE MOVER 3000** stopped moving. I perked up my ears, but I didn't hear anything. I leaned over and very **slowwwwwwly** opened the porthole.

"**WOW!**" Professor von Volt shouted.

"**WOW!**" I shouted.

"**WOW!**" Thea shouted.

"**WOW!**" Benjamin shouted.

"**SWEET!**" Trap shouted.

The Egyptian desert stretched for miles and miles in every direction around us. It was a sea of golden sand as fine as powder, gently shaped into **softly** angled dunes. The rising sun tinged the pyramids and the Sphinx with a **rosy** hue.

"Look!" Benjamin exclaimed in AMAZEMENT. "The pyramids are white and have golden tips! And the Sphinx is painted in different colors!"

I made a note in my travel journal: *It is 1280*

Egyptian society was arranged in this hierarchy.

BC at 5:47 A.M. We're in Giza, in the middle of the Egyptian desert.

The professor rummaged in his pockets and took out some TEENY TINY clothes.

"This is what we'll wear while we're in Egypt!" he told us. "I put these clothes through a special *miniaturization* process before we left."

He took from his pocket a little test tube full of **transparent** liquid and used an eyedropper to splash one drop of the strange substance on a LiTTLe piece of clothing. The tiny dress **grew** into a pleated linen dress, complete with a wig.

The professor gave it to Thea, along with a small GILDED wooden box. In it were **expensive** perfumes and alabaster vases filled with ancient Egyptian makeup.

After we dressed, Thea put eye makeup on all of us. Now we really looked like ancient Egyptians!

I noticed Trap put something in his bag. It

looked like a little **BLACK** fabric pouch.

"Oh!" the professor exclaimed suddenly, slapping his forehead. "I almost forgot!" He took out a tiny earpiece. "This is a Squeak Speak, a special translator I invented," he told us. "It can translate everything you hear and all that you say!"

Trap popped a Squeak Speak in his ear. "It doesn't work." he said. "I don't hear anything!"

"Of course you don't!" Professor von

MAKEUP

Egyptians applied makeup around their eyes for aesthetic reasons and to protect themselves from the sun's rays and from damage from the sandy desert winds. The most popular colors were black and green. The Egyptians mixed a blue-gray mineral called galena with soot to make black eye makeup. Green eye makeup was made from malachite, a bright green copper ore.

Volt replied with a sigh. "You have to turn it on first!"

Trap turned on the device. "One, two, three, TESTIIIIIIIIIING!" he squealed loudly. "Geronimo, do you hear MEEEEEEEEE?"

"Shhh!" Thea shushed Trap. "Listen!"

From far away, I heard mice chanting:

"OUR DAYS ARE LONG, OUR WORK IS TOUGH, BUILDING TEMPLES IS REALLY ROUGH. WE'LL KEEP WORKING TILL THE DAY IS DONE. TO HONOR RA, GOD OF THE SUN. WE ARE PROUD AND WE ARE STRONG, WE'LL WORK FOR MAAT ALL DAY LONG."

It was a group of laborers going to work.

"Unbelievable!" I whispered in amazement. "I can understand ancient Egyptian!"

"What's *Maat*, Professor?" Benjamin asked.

"Maat is the DIVINE ORDER," Professor

von Volt replied. "According to the ancient Egyptians, the whole world follows the law of universal order and balance. And Ra is the sun god the Egyptians adored."

We hid the **MOUSE MOVER 3000** in a hole in the sand and covered it with palm leaves. Then we got to work. Thea snapped some **PHOTOS**, I took NOTES, and Benjamin and the professor took samples of sand and sealed them in plastic *bags*. Trap lay **LAZILY** in the shadow of the Sphinx, napping.

After an hour, we were all done.

"Where are we going for breakfast?" Trap asked, **YAWNING** loudly. "I just can't get moving without a nice cup of **COFFEE** in the morning!"

THE GREAT PYRAMID OF GIZA

Suddenly, we heard a noise. We ran and hid behind the **GREAT PYRAMID OF GIZA**.

ANCIENT EGYPTIAN GODS

Nephthys, goddess of death

Nut, goddess of the sky

Geb, god of the Earth

Atum, the first god

Shu, god of air

Tefnut, goddess of rain

Khnum, god of rebirth and creation

Anubis, god of the afterlife

Sekhmet, warrior goddess

Ra, sun god

Sobek, crocodile god

Thoth, ibis god

Khepri, god of the scarab beetle

Hathor, goddess of motherhood

Set, god of the desert

Bastet, cat goddess

Osiris, god of the afterlife

Isis, goddess of nature and magic

Horus, god of war and hunting

ARREST THOSE RODENTS!

A **LOOOOONG** procession of soldiers carrying a **golden** litter with silky curtains came into view.

"Make way for the Grand Vizier, the **NOBLE MOUSEHOTEP!**" the soldiers shouted.

The curtains parted and I glimpsed a sly-looking, shifty-eyed rat. He was wearing a white linen robe and a blue lapis lazuli necklace decorated with a large gold scarab beetle. He wore a black

wig woven with silver threads and pearls, and his tail was decorated with rings made of precious stones.

His servants placed the litter *gently* on the ground, and the rat climbed out of the *ornate* chair. A servant ran to him and placed a pair of **golden** sandals on his paws.

Mousehotep nibbled DAINTILY on a bunch of grapes. Meanwhile, Trap took out a piece of garlic chewing gum and waved it in front of my nose.

"Want some?" he whispered.

"Shhh!" I shushed him. "You know I'm allergic to garlic. Ah . . . ah . . . ah . . . **achoo**!"

I sneezed.

The Noble Mousehotep heard me.

"**Scampering scarabs!**" he cried. "Arrest those rodents! They are tomb thieves. Scribe, write that down!"

The soldiers surrounded us, poking at us with their **SPEARS**, while the scribe **SCRIBBLED** something on a piece of papyrus.

RAMESSES! RAMESSES! RAMESSES!

The head guard forced us to march through the extremely **HOT** desert for what seemed to be an **eternity**! Finally, we arrived at the royal palace of Memphis.

The guard **poked** me in the tail with his lance.

"Bow before the pharaoh!" he ordered me.

At the very far end of the great hall, which was

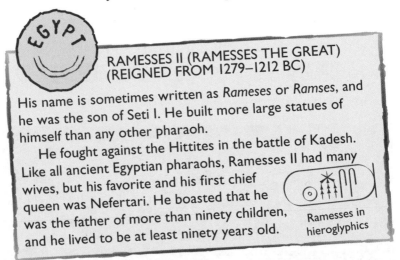

EGYPT

RAMESSES II (RAMESSES THE GREAT) (REIGNED FROM 1279–1212 BC)

His name is sometimes written as *Rameses* or *Ramses*, and he was the son of Seti I. He built more large statues of himself than any other pharaoh.

He fought against the Hittites in the battle of Kadesh. Like all ancient Egyptian pharaohs, Ramesses II had many wives, but his favorite and his first chief queen was Nefertari. He boasted that he was the father of more than ninety children, and he lived to be at least ninety years old.

Ramesses in hieroglyphics

decorated in **MAGNIFICENT** frescoes, I saw a **golden** throne.

A tall, thin rodent with a hooked nose and hawk-like eyes sat on the throne. It was Ramesses II!

Two tall mice stood on either side of the throne, fanning the pharaoh with **ENORMOUSE** ostrich feathers. The pharaoh wore a **double** crown — part red, part white — symbolizing his dominion over Upper and Lower Egypt. He proudly held a **gold** scepter in his paw.

Queen Nefertari was seated next to him. She was **gorgeous**! He looked at her proudly; you could tell he was very much in **love** with her. Next to the royal couple was their daughter. In her arms, she held a little bundle wrapped in a blanket **EMBROIDERED** in gold. It was the little baby **Moses***!

The pharaoh's daughter with little baby Moses

---

* In Hebrew, *Moses* means "savior" or "drawn out from the water." In Egyptian, it means "son" or "child."

NOBLE MOUSEHOTEP'S SARCOPHAGUS

Grand Vizier Mousehotep **BOWED** before Ramesses.

"Honor to you, **Pharaoh**!" he squeaked. "I wish you life, strength, and health!"

Then he turned to the scribe. "Read!" he ordered.

The scribe read **aloud**:

"HIGH PHARAOH 🐊, SON OF THE SUN ☀, RA'S PRIDE, I 🔺 SURPRISED THESE FIVE RODENTS 🐭🐭🐭🐭🐭 BEHIND THE PYRAMID 🔺 OF CHEOPS. THEY ARE MUMMY 🧟 THIEVES. LET'S FEED THEM TO THE CROCODILES 🐊!"

The pharaoh stared at us with a look of FIRE in his eyes. When he finally spoke, his voice was so deep and scary it made me shiver with fright!

"Is this true?" he asked us.

Professor von Volt stepped forward and bowed.

"Noble Ramesses II, we are innocent!" he said.

The Noble Mousehotep laughed an EVIL laugh.

"INNOCENT?" he scoffed. "Everyone says that. To the crocodiles, I say! Did you get that, scribe?"

The scribe chuckled.

"I got it, boss!" he replied.

But the pharaoh lifted a paw.

"If you're not THIEVES, then what are you?" he asked us.

"Pharaoh Ramesses, we are TRAVELERS from afar,"

WOMEN

Women had a lot of liberty in ancient Egypt compared to many early societies: They could work and choose whom to wed. Women could even be pharaohs — Hatshepsut, the fifth pharaoh of the eighteenth dynasty, was female and is thought to have been one of the most successful pharaohs in ancient Egypt.

The pharaoh's dinner

Musicians

Dancers

Scrolls of papyrus

Scribe

Mousehotep

Pool

Guards

Servants

Nefertari   Ramesses II

the professor explained. "We have knowledge of many **SECRETS**. . . ."

"You must be **magicians**!" Nefertari squeaked with excitement.

Trap took advantage of the situation and threw himself at the foot of her **Throne**.

"Oh yes, we are magicians," he said. "And we're really, really good ones!"

Trap pulled on a black cloak with a **silky** scarlet lining. Then he rummaged around in his **mysterious** satin pouch. He clapped his paws, and instantly a **WHITE** dove appeared out of thin air and settled on Nefertari's shoulders.

The queen squeaked with delight.

Next, Trap produced a top hat. Out of the hat **POPPED** two tiny white rabbit ears.

Trap clapped his paws. . . .

Flap
Flap

"You get back in there," Trap grunted. "I don't want you yet!"

It turned out that Trap's satin pouch contained everything a mouse needed for a **magic show!**

"Come one, come all," Trap shouted loudly. "Come be amazed by the magic of the **Great** and **Powerful** Trappolik Who Came from Afar! He'll make objects mysteriously **appear** and **disappear**, and he will saw in half the most reckless volunteer — er, I mean, ahem, the most **courageous** volunteer!"

He waved a silk scarf in front of the pharaoh's scepter, and it disappeared instantly! Six soldiers rushed toward him, but in an instant, Trap made the scepter **appear** again.

"**VOILA!**" Trap squeaked triumphantly.

Everyone held their breath.

He made the pharaoh's scepter disappear!

Then Ramesses chuckled. **"HEE, HEE, HEE!"** Everyone laughed with him. "Hee, hee, hee!"

"I need a box!" Trap squeaked loudly. "Never mind, I found one."

He dragged a **sarcophagus** covered in gold and precious stones in front of the throne.

"You're about to see the world's most **SPECTACULAR** demonstration!" Trap announced boldly.

"Hey!" the Noble Mousehotep protested. "Let go of that sarcophagus. It's mine! And it's very precious!"

But Ramesses nodded for Trap to continue with the show.

Mousehotep began to **sob** uncontrollably.

"That sarcophagus cost me a **FORTUNE!**"

he whined. "Write that down, scribe!"

"Got it, boss!" the scribe replied.

"Ladies and gentlemice, I will now saw my cousin in **HALF**," Trap announced. "Oh, what am I saying? I'm going to saw him in **THIRDS**, no, in **QUARTERS**. Yes, quarters. After all, I'm feeling **good** today."

I began to **sweat** profusely.

"Why me?" I squeaked.

Trap pulled me by the tail.

"Oh, come on," he insisted. "You've got the **easiest** part!"

Then he tripped me and locked me in the sarcophagus.

"**HELP!**" I yelled. "I'm afraid of closed spaces. Trap, let me out, I tell you! I'm **CLAUSTROPHOBIC**!"

"Oh, you'll be fine!" Trap

replied with a chuckle. "Don't you $trust$ me?"

"Of course not!" I mumbled from inside the sarcophagus, but Trap didn't hear me.

He began *sawing* and *whistling* at the same time.

"Don't worry, Geronimo," Trap said. "I've tried this trick a DOZEN times. It almost always works!"

It almost always works!

After a few seconds, Trap stopped sawing. "Voila!" he announced. "I've sliced my cousin!"

I reached down to feel my tail. I was still **INTACT**!

Trap opened the sarcophagus and I jumped out. I was as pale as a slice of **mozzarella**. The court applauded with enthusiasm.

"**Bravoooo!**" the mice shouted. "More! More!"

"Pharaoh, who's going to fix my sarcophagus?" Mousehotep demanded as he wiped his tears.

"Quiet!" Ramesses hissed. "Don't bother the **GREAT** and Powerful Trappolik Who Came from Afar!"

"Yeah!" Trap agreed with a nod of his head. "Don't bother the **Great** and POWERFUL Trappolik Who Came from Afar!"

Mousehotep glared at my cousin.

"By all the sphinxes in Egypt, I'll get you!" he grumbled under his breath. **"WRITE THAT DOWN, SCRIBE!"**

"Got it, boss!" the scribe replied.

Got it, boss!

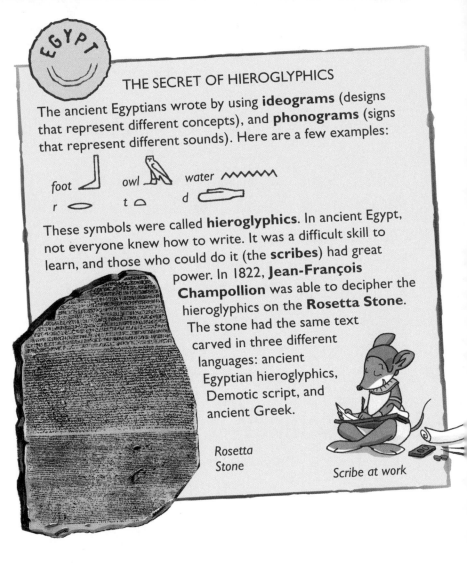

EGYPT

THE SECRET OF HIEROGLYPHICS

The ancient Egyptians wrote by using **ideograms** (designs that represent different concepts), and **phonograms** (signs that represent different sounds). Here are a few examples:

foot   owl   water ∿∿∿∿

r   t   d

These symbols were called **hieroglyphics**. In ancient Egypt, not everyone knew how to write. It was a difficult skill to learn, and those who could do it (the **scribes**) had great power. In 1822, **Jean-François Champollion** was able to decipher the hieroglyphics on the **Rosetta Stone**. The stone had the same text carved in three different languages: ancient Egyptian hieroglyphics, Demotic script, and ancient Greek.

Rosetta Stone

Scribe at work

This is how you write *Geronimo* in Egyptian:

Now use the key on the next page to try to write your own name!

EGYPTIAN ALPHABET

In reality, there was no Egyptian alphabet. This is an approximation of what the Egyptian alphabet might have looked like.

A	🦅	J		S	
B		K		T	
C		L		U	
D		M		V	
E	/	N	⌇	W	
F		O		X	
G		P	▢	Y	
H		Q		Z	
I		R			

EGYPTIAN NUMBERS

1		10	∩	100	ℓ	1,000	
2	‖	20	∩∩	200	ℓℓ	10,000	
3	⦀	30	∩∩∩	300	ℓℓℓ	100,000	
4	⦀|	40	∩∩∩∩	400	ℓℓℓℓ	1,000,000	

Ooooooooooh . . . Magic!

The pharaoh had been so impressed with Trap's magic show that he invited us to stay instead of throwing us to the **crocodiles**. The Egyptians were about to have a **FEAST**.

"Let the celebration in honor of Hapi begin!" Ramesses announced.

I realized he was referring to the flooding of the River Nile, which the Egyptians revered and called **HAPI**.

The priests dressed all in white and lit sticks of perfumed incense. Seven dancers wearing **golden-threaded** wigs and **LAPIS LAZULI** necklaces entered the great hall. They danced as they shook the sistrum and tossed rose petals into the air. Then they somersaulted gracefully around

The sistrum was an ancient Egyptian percussion instrument.

the pool in the center of the hall, which was filled with water lilies.

Meanwhile, the musicians played **sweet** melodies on the harp, cithara, lyre, lute, castanets, and tambourines.

The servants set out a meal of QUAIL, roasted meat, goat cheese, **spicy** beans, pomegranates, grapes, caramelized nuts, honey, and fig marmalade on alabaster dishes.

Ramesses popped a honey treat in his mouth. Suddenly, he groaned in **pain**.

"Oh, ouch!" he cried. "**Ouchie**! Ouchie! Ouch!"

"Poor **dear**, does your tooth ache?" Nefertari SQUEAKED.

MEDICINE

Egyptian doctors knew how to mend bone fractures, how to drill into the skull, and how to perform complicated surgeries. They also cured some illnesses with certain types of mold, which is the active ingredient in modern-day penicillin. The Egyptians filled cavities with a special cement and tied false teeth to real ones with golden threads.

A gold mirror

"Oh, yes," he sighed, rubbing his cheek. "I've really got to go to the dentist!"

The festivities were about to begin, and a servant brought Nefertari a **golden** mirror studded with **RUBIES** so she could freshen her makeup.

Unfortunately, the mirror was clouded over and couldn't **REFLECT** very much.

Trap took note of this and rummaged around in his pouch. He took out a sparkling new mirror. Then he bowed down and offered it to the queen. She gasped in wonder.

"Ooooooooh . . . magic!" she exclaimed.

Nefertari gave Trap the **SWEETEST** smile.

"He's phenomenal. . . ." I heard one of the other mice whisper.

"A **TRUE** magician, and a whisker-licking good one at that," another replied.

"It seems he comes from very **far** away," a third WHISPERED. "He must be very **powerful**."

"Yes, very powerful," the first agreed. "Maybe more powerful than the pharaoh . . ."

"Mm-hmmm," the second said. "The queen smiled at him. . . ."

"Ramesses must be so jealous!" another chimed in.

Mummified mozzarella! We were in big **trouble** if those mice were correct. It wasn't a good idea to make the pharaoh jealous. Mousehotep whispered something in the pharaoh's ear. Ramesses **NARROWED** his eyes and **curled** the tips of his mustache in a way that made my whiskers **tremble** in fear.

EGYPT

CLOTHING

Wealthy Egyptians wore pleated linen skirts and tunics that were tinted with vegetable dye, while shepherds and farmers wore tunics made of rough animal skins. Tunics were rarely made of wool. The rich wore leather sandals, while the poor wore sandals made of woven straw.

Ouch! Who Pinched Me?

Ramesses stormed out of the hall looking very, very ANGRY. Mousehotep followed closely behind, whispering to Ramesses and shooting us dirty looks.

I knew it! I knew we were in **trouble**!

"I told you the pharaoh was jealous. . . ." I heard a mouse murmur.

"It serves that **magician** right!" said another.

"Mm-hmmm," agreed a third. "Ramesses will feed him to the crocodiles for sure!"

"By tomorrow, the only thing left of him and his

Hee, hee, hee!

friends will be their TiNY LiTTLe BoNeS!"

Holey cheese! We were doomed!

Mousehotep came running into the main hall. "Guards, imprison the strangers!" he shouted with delight. "Pharaoh's orders!"

Before I could **SQUEAK** a reply, we were surrounded. The guards poked us with their lances and we were led to the palace's **DUNGEON**.

"Hee, hee, hee!" Mousehotep chuckled. "You thought you were being so **CLEVER**, but now you'll pay **DEARLY** for your insolence."

He poked Trap's chubby tummy.

"Oh, yes!" he cackled. "The King of the Sacred Crocodiles is going to love you!"

"Look here," my cousin protested, placing a paw

on his round belly. "This is pure MUSCLE!"

Trap, Thea, Benjamin, Professor von Volt, and I settled into our dank, **dark** cell.

I climbed up on the lone **WOODEN** bench and looked out the small prison window. Right in front of me was a muddy pool of water. In it swam gigantic, hungry-looking crocodiles.

Why, why, oh, why had I agreed to come on this wacky journey through time?

Suddenly, something pinched my tail.

"Ouch!" I exclaimed. "Who's that? Who's there? Who pinched me?"

It wasn't the pharaoh's soldiers, but a LOVELY maiden.

"Shhh!" she whispered. "Follow me, all of you. And be quiet!"

We scurried away through a DARK passageway. SMOKY torches cast an eerie glow on the walls, which were covered in hieroglyphics. The maiden led us to an enormouse statue of Sobek, the **frightening** crocodile god. She pressed the statue's left paw, and the statue revolved to reveal a **SECRET** door.

We **followed** the maiden through the door and found ourselves in the queen's **PRIVATE** chambers!

Nefertari **RAN** toward us, a **worried** look on her snout.

"You have to get away!" she said urgently. "The pharaoh is **very** jealous!"

"But why are you helping us?" Thea asked the queen suspiciously.

Nefertari turned **PURPLE** with embarrassment.

"Sometimes the pharaoh can be a real bully," she admitted. "He's especially **GRUMPY** right now because of his awful toothache. You seem like decent mice. You should have a chance to **ESCAPE**."

"Thank you," I told her gratefully. "We will remember your **KiNDNeSS**."

The queen removed one of her **PRECIOUS** rings and gave it to Trap.

This ring will protect you!

"Here," she told him. "This ring will protect you. **TRaVeL SafeLy!**"

Let's Go! Roooooooooow!

The maiden told us to lie down on a giant **woven** rug. Then she **rolled** up the rug, hiding us inside. Some servants carried us straight to the port in Memphis. It was already five o'clock in the afternoon.

"**Crusty cheese curds!**" Trap mumbled. "I missed lunch. I don't like this at all!"

I heard the sound of **waves** lapping against the shore. I stuck my snout out of the rug. We had been loaded onto a felucca, a small wooden boat propelled by oars and sails.

"Mummified mozzarella and

Captain Sewer al-Rati

petrified papyrus!" we heard an **ANGRY** voice shout. "This is the laziest crew since Atum created Egypt! We have to get up the Nile before sunset. Let's go! **ROOOOOOW!**"

Captain Sewer al-Rati was a **MUSCULAR** rat with **curly** whiskers. He wore a rough linen skirt and wide leather bracelets on his wrists.

"One pyramid, two pyramids, three pyramids, **ROW**! One pyramid, two pyramids, three pyramids, **ROW**!"

Everyone rowed vigorously. The ship left the Memphis port and began to sail down the river. I was **green** with seasickness. The boat went **UP** and **DOWN**, **UP** and **DOWN**, and **UP** and **DOWN**. I felt like I was going to toss my cheese!

Why, why, oh, why had I agreed to come on this wacky journey through time?

LOOK OUT FOR HIPPOS!

We had been traveling for several hours, and night had fallen.

Suddenly, a sailor shouted: "Look out for hippopotamuses!"

Hippopotamuses? What hippopotamuses?

Another sailor shouted, "Petrified papyrus! They're **ENORMOUSE**! And there are a lot of them!"

I felt faint. *Enormouse hippos?*

Captain Sewer al-Rati thundered: "Scampering scarabs . . . WE'RE SINKING!"

My whiskers twisted from fright. **SINKING?**

Suddenly, the ship began to tilt **wildly** to one side.

"Mummified mozzarella!" I squeaked. "We'll be **dinner** for those hungry hippos!"

Why, why, oh, why had I agreed to come on this wacky journey through time?

A huge wave crashed against the side of the boat. The boat was filling with water *fast*.

I grabbed a basket full of fish and dumped them overboard. Then I started scooping up basketfuls of water.

"Hurry," I urged my friends. "We have to bail out the boat!"

But it was no use. The water just seeped out the sides of the basket!

"Farewell, friends!" I cried out to the professor, Trap, Thea, and Benjamin. "We're sinking!"

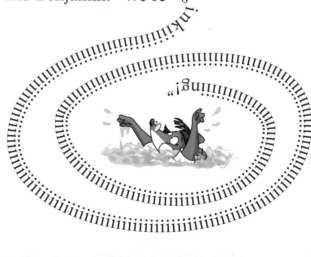

SNIP, SNIP, SNAP!

A moment later, I found myself in the **muddy** waters of the Nile River. I fumbled and thrashed, trying to keep my snout above **water**. But my soaked linen garment was pulling me down.

"**Crusty cheese curds**," I heard my cousin grumble. "Now I've missed dinner, too!"

In the light of the full moon, I saw lots of shiny dots SHIMMERING in the dark. Trembling, I realized they were CROCODILE eyes!

"Crocs!" I yelled to my friends. "Swim!"

With the crocodiles nipping at our tails, we swam toward the shore. SNIP, SNIP, SNAP!

One of the crocodiles BIT Trap on the tail.

"Ouchie, ouchie, ouch!" Trap yelled. He

grabbed an oar and waved it at the crocodile.

The crocodile snapped at Trap.

Trap poked the crocodile with the oar and began to sing.

"Stay back, stay back, you crusty old croc!
You smell like a pair of three-day-old socks.
Your sickening smell is worse than your bite.
So go away, scram — get out of our sight!"

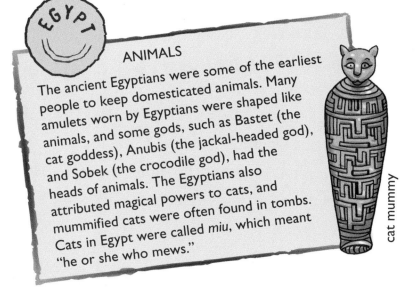

ANIMALS

The ancient Egyptians were some of the earliest people to keep domesticated animals. Many amulets worn by Egyptians were shaped like animals, and some gods, such as Bastet (the cat goddess), Anubis (the jackal-headed god), and Sobek (the crocodile god), had the heads of animals. The Egyptians also attributed magical powers to cats, and mummified cats were often found in tombs. Cats in Egypt were called *miu*, which meant "he or she who mews."

cat mummy

THE BEST NIGHT
OF MY LIFE!

Luckily, we made it to shore. The moonlight **illuminated** the white beach, and the thick papyrus growing along the shore **SWAYED** in the night breeze. Suddenly, I saw a shadow among the papyrus fronds, and something hit me on the head. *Bonk!*

OOOOOUCHIE! WHAT A BLOW, WHAT A WHACK, WHAT A WALLOP!

As I passed out, I heard Trap **grumbling** in the background.

"Geronimo is always the same," he said. "He'll do anything to get attention. There he goes, fainting again!"

A few seconds later, I came to. A **tiny** figure stood in front of me. It was a little mouse about the same age as Benjamin.

She had a shaved head except for a thick braid that was decorated with a little PAINTED wooden ball. She wore an antelope skin that was tied at her waist by a BRAIDED leather belt.

"Are you still alive?" she squeaked anxiously. "I'm so sorry! I hit you with my **throwing stick**!"

Professor von Volt was scribbling notes.

"Interesting," he mused. "This Egyptian throwing stick is identical to the boomerang used by Australian Aboriginals!"

Pa-rat Riri-rat Ma-rat

The LiTTLe mouse told us her name was Riri-rat. She took us to a mud hut where her parents welcomed us **WARMLY**. Pa-rat invited us to stay.

"No one in my village will ever go through the night hungry!" he said, using an ancient Egyptian proverb.

"It's about time we had something to **eat**!" Trap announced as he patted his belly and licked his lips.

The family offered us everything they had with a smile: dried fish, fresh cucumbers, fava beans with garlic, barley cakes made with sesame oil, goat cheese, and ripe, juicy figs.

We sat in a circle on WOVEN mats and ate the food with our paws.

After we ate, the adult mice played **senet** while Benjamin and Riri-rat played with a toy maze. Even though we were in a mud hut LIT by an oil lamp almost 3,300 years in the past, it was the *best* night of my life. The food was simple and delicious, and it was offered with **warmth** and generosity!

We chatted about many things and made the most of the PEACEFUL, relaxing evening.

I turned to our hosts.

"Friends, tomorrow we must secretly return to Giza," I told them. "We've escaped our captors but we need to complete our mission."

Benjamin looked sad about leaving.

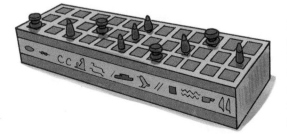

Senet was a game similar to backgammon. It was played on a rectangular board with thirty-six squares.

Benjamin and Riri-rat's maze

● FINISH

"The memory of this charming night will live in our 𝕙𝕖𝕒𝕣𝕥𝕤 forever!" I assured everyone.

Even though we were very different from Riri-rat and her family, we were united by friendship. It was **comforting** to know that no matter how far we had traveled through time, we had found true friends who had warmed our hearts with their hospitality.

There is no greater gift than friendship!

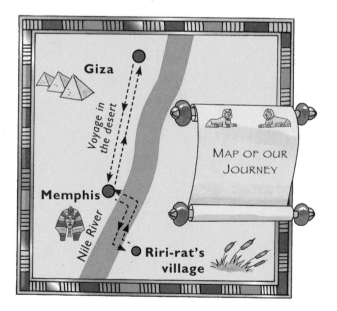

THE MUMMY'S CAFÉ

That night, we slept on pallets made of **DRIED** grass. At dawn, we went down to the river with Pa-rat and helped him bring in the night's catch: a netful of **fish**. We explained to him that we had to quickly return to Memphis and from there, travel back to Giza. We also told him no one was to know of our plans. If Ramesses or Mousehotep found us, we would be in **BIG** trouble!

Pa-rat put his paw over his **heart**.

"You have my word of honor," he squeaked. "I will be as silent as an **OBELISK**! But you'll need a guide."

Suddenly, a small, chubby fisherman appeared from behind a dune. He had a **sly** look on his snout.

"Oh, oh!" Pa-rat whispered. "That's

Obelisk

Chatty al-Mousi, the town gossip!"

Chatty cleared his throat.

"Erhem," he said. "Pardon me, but I was just passing by when I heard you needed a **guide**. My brother's cousin's uncle's maid's niece's scribe's sister's embalmer's grandfather is a tourist guide in Memphis. His name is **BAB-BEOT**. You'll find him at the port, at **THE MUMMY'S CAFÉ**. I'll send him a carrier pigeon to let him know you're coming."

Since we didn't have any other options, we agreed. Pa-rat helped us build a **boat**. We would glide up the Nile to Memphis.

Just as we were about to leave, Riri-rat gave Benjamin her throwing stick.

"It's the most **valuable** thing I have," she told him. "That's why I want to give it to you.

We gathered and cut lots of papyrus plants and tied them together with sturdy knots to make a boat.

I wish you a peaceful and safe journey."

She kissed him sweetly on the cheek. Benjamin's snout turned **PURPLE** with embarrassment. He's a **shy** mouse, just like me. We boarded the raft and waved good-bye. The raft slowly **glided** on the river.

After a few hours, the current began to **whirl**. We were getting closer and closer to the rapids. The boat began to pick up **SPEED**.

"We should slow down!" I yelled to Trap.

"No way!" Trap replied. "You're such a **scaredy**-mouse. Now comes the fun part!"

He steered the boat right into the rapids.

"Wheeeeeeeeeee!" he shouted.

As I was tossed UP and DOWN and UP and DOWN and UP and DOWN among the waves, panic took hold of me. I grabbed the sides of the boat. Suddenly, a branch fell off a tree near the shore. It hit me on the head. **BONK!**

Ooooouchie! What a blow, what a whack, what a wallop!

As I passed out, I heard Trap grumbling in the background.

"Geronimo is always the same," he said. "He'll do anything to get attention. Look, he fainted again!"

The evening of the second day, we arrived in Memphis. We tied up the boat right near the entrance to the port.

Then we quickly made our way to the Mummy's Café.

When we entered, a short, skinny bald rat greeted us. He shouted loudly.

"Hi, there!" he said. "Are you the ones who want to go to Giza?"

The professor tried to QUIET him.

"Shhh!" he said. "Please speak SOFTLY or we'll be discovered!"

"Discovered?" he shouted back, louder than before. "Discover what? Is there a SECRET? A very secret secret? Huh? Is there?"

We ushered him to a quiet table in the back of the café, hoping no one had heard him.

"My name is BaB-BeOt," he introduced himself. "It means 'brain lice of the desert.' But I have other names, too. Like

brain lice of the desert

Kiak-Kie-Rom, which means 'My tongue is longer than that of a horned viper.' I'm also known as **Mum-Puz**, which means 'My paws stink worse than a rotting mummy,' as well as *Atten al-Alit*, or 'My breath is fouler than that of a garlic-eating jackal.'"

My tongue is longer than that of a horned viper

My paws stink worse than a rotting mummy

My breath is fouler than that of a garlic-eating jackal

Professor von Volt took a step backward. The guide truly had **stinky** breath.

"Ahem, can we get going?" Thea asked. "We're in a hurry to get to Giza."

"Don't you want to first go on a *beautiful* cruise down the Nile?" the guide asked us.

"No, thank you," Benjamin replied. "We want to go to Giza!"

"You could visit the tomb of King —"

"Maybe another time," Thea replied PATIENTLY. "We want to go to Giza!"

"Want to see the Temple of Ptah? There's a **golden** statue of Seti I, our pharaoh's dad. . . ."

"Nope!" Trap replied in frustration. "We want to go to Giza! G-i-z-a! **GIZAAAAAAAAAA!**"

"Oh, you want to go to **Giza**?" the guide asked. "Why didn't you say so? All right, let's go to Giza, then. But I don't know what you want to see there. There are only three **pyramids**

Why didn't you say so?

and a **SPHINX** in Giza. But if that's where you want to go, I'll take you. **Mummified mozzarella!** You only had to say so!"

THE TEMPLE OF THE EMBALMERS

We left the café to find mice had gathered in the street to celebrate. We had made it to Memphis just in time. The Nile River had begun to overflow, and everyone was celebrating since the FLOODING guarantees an abundant harvest.

Bab-beot signaled us to follow him.

"Let's go," he told us. "Here's the HOUSE OF LiFE, the temple where embalmers prepare the dead for eternal life. Do you want to see it?"

SCAMPERING SCARABS! I didn't want to see any mummies — I'm a big scaredy-mouse!

But he had already opened the heavy door, and I couldn't help but look inside. My head began to spin, and I started to sweat.

"How are you feeling, Uncle?" Benjamin

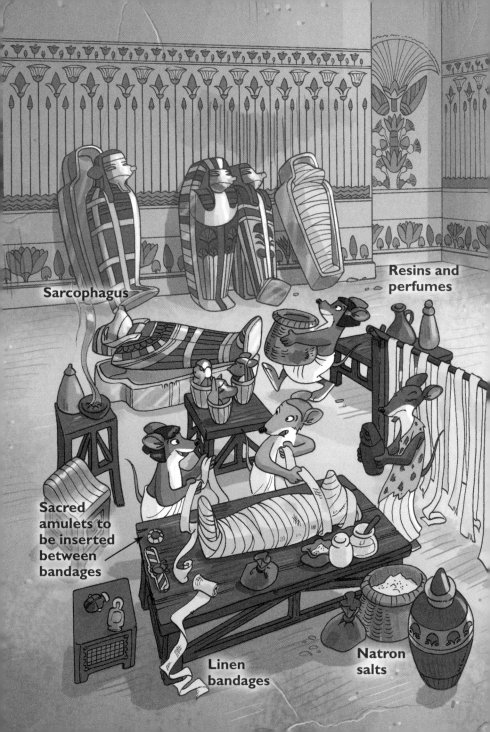

Sarcophagus

Resins and
perfumes

Sacred
amulets to
be inserted
between
bandages

Linen
bandages

Natron
salts

Funeral mask

Mummy

Brazier

Canopic jars

EMBALMING

After the body was washed, the priests took a hook and extracted the brain through the nose. The internal organs were also extracted and preserved in **canopic jars**. The body was immersed in natron salt for forty days until it was completely dehydrated. Then the body was coated in a layer of **resin and perfumes**. After that, the body was wrapped tightly in linen bandages. **Precious amulets** were tucked between layers of bandages. These amulets were said to protect the body in the afterlife. A **funeral mask** replicating the features of the deceased was placed on the mummy's face. Finally, the mummy was placed in a **sarcophagus**.

The Egyptians believed that if they preserved the body of the deceased, the soul would find rest and live for eternity. So mummies were entombed along with everything they would need in the afterlife, including **food**, **furniture**, and little statues called **ushabti** that were intended to act as substitutes for the mummy in case he or she was made to do manual labor in the afterlife.

Unfortunately, thieves raided many Egyptian tombs and many treasures have been lost. One of the most interesting tombs was that of the pharaoh **Tutankhamen**, which was almost completely intact when it was discovered in 1922 by archaeologists **Howard Carter** and **George Herbert**.

whispered. "You're as pale as a slice of mozzarella!"

I leaned against a **marble** column. The column tipped over and hit a sarcophagus. Then the lid hit me on the head. **BONK!**

Ooouchie! What a blow, what a whack, what a wallop!

Before I passed out, I heard my cousin's voice.

"Geronimo is always the same," Trap grumbled. "He'll do anything to get attention. There he goes, fainting again!"

I leaned against a marble column . . .

. . . but the column fell . . .

. . . and hit a sarcophagus.

The lid hit me on the head!

Bonk!

ARE WE THERE YET?

When I came to, Benjamin was fanning me with a palm leaf.

"It's all right, Uncle G," Benjamin said *sweetly*. "Everything will be okay. I'm right here."

It was still dark, but we began our *TREK* across the desert. We walked and walked and walked.

Just before dawn, Bab-beot suddenly stopped.

"Mummified mozzarella, I've got a great idea!" he told us. "Why don't we take a SHORTCUT?"

"But isn't it DANGEROUS to leave the road?" Benjamin asked, a worried look on his snout.

"No, no, no, it's fine," Bab-beot replied. "You have me as a guide! I've practically memorized a complete map of the entire Sahara desert!"

The sun began to rise. At ten in the MORNING it was BURNING, by eleven it was SCORCHING, and by noon it was really, really scalding!

"Are we there yet?" Thea asked Bab-beot.

"By the shadow of the sphinx, we'll be there in a bit," he replied with a sigh.

Two hours later, Thea asked him again.

"Are we there yet??"

"By all the stones in the pyramids, we're almost there!"

Three hours later, Thea asked again.

"Are we there yet???"

"By the light of the rising sun, we're just about there!"

Thea grabbed Bab-beot by the tail. "We've been here before! I remember this rock!"

Professor von Volt stepped between Thea and our guide.

"Okay, Bab-beot," the professor said politely but firmly. "Tell us the **TRUTH**!"

He burst into tears.

"By the curly whiskers of the pharaoh's great-grandfather, I'm afraid I'm lost!"

A tomb-like silence fell over the group. I began to panic, which made me VERY thirsty.

"Trap, please pass me a little water," I whispered.

"WATER?" He paled. "Didn't *you* bring it?"

"No," I replied. "You told me you were going to take care of the provisions."

"I did," Trap said. "I packed the **dried** herring, salted beef, and brined hot peppers. But I didn't take any water."

"All salty things?" I shouted back. "And no water? What were you thinking?!"

Why, why, oh, why had I agreed to come on this wacky journey through time?

We took refuge under the shade of the first palm tree we found. Once the SUN had slipped behind the sand dunes, Professor von Volt opened his bag and took out a BRASS instrument.

"It's a SEXTANT. It will be useful for helping us figure out where we are." He pointed the instrument toward the sky.

"We're very close to Giza!" he announced **HAPPILY**. "Just a few more hours, and we'll be there!"

The sextant is an optical instrument that can measure the distance from the horizon to a star in the sky. This measurement can then be used to determine one's location.

Put Your Paw Here, Cousin!

By dawn, we were **exhausted**. We had been walking across the desert for more than twenty-four hours! And we hadn't had a drop of water to drink! Benjamin was slowly **dragging** his little paws through the sand. I hoisted him onto my back and began the trudge again.

"Uncle . . . Uncle Geronimo . . ." he whispered.

"What is it, my little **CHEESE NIP**?" I asked, my mouth bone-dry.

Benjamin didn't answer. He just pointed his finger toward the horizon. I took off my glasses and polished them on the sleeve of my jacket. When I put them back on, I saw something ahead. But what was it? Maybe it was a **MIRAGE**, but I thought I saw the giant sphinx of Giza. And

behind the sphinx was an **OASIS**!

With our last bit of remaining strength, we dragged ourselves toward the cluster of palms, sycamores, and tamarinds, where a spring of CRYSTAL CLEAR water flowed.

"Water . . . water . . . water!" Trap stammered as he dove into the pool of water.

"How's your nephew, Geronimo?" Professor von Volt asked.

"He'll be FINE, Professor," I replied.

I carried Benjamin to the spring, and helped him take a drink. Then I gave him a tiny kiss ♥ on top of his head.

"We're saved, little one," I told him. "Saved!"

Once he'd had his fill, I took a drink myself. I drank and drank and drank. Ah, how good water tastes when one is thirsty!

Once we had all had our fill of water, I realized how **HUNGRY** I was. I could have eaten twenty

WHEELS of cheese all by myself!

Faster than a cat chasing a rat, Trap hopped out of the water and **SCAMPERED** up a palm tree. A minute later, a bunch of dates fell on my head. **Bonk!**

Ooouchie! What a blow, what a whack, what a wallop!

My head began to **SPIN** and my paws started to **sweat**. As I passed out, I heard my cousin grumbling.

"Geronimo is always the same," Trap said. "He'll do anything to get attention. There he goes, fainting again!"

Finally, I came to.

We were excited to be back in Giza at last. But our good mood was cut short when we heard someone **sobbing** nearby.

"Oh, may the scarabs **save** me!" a voice squeaked. "What will the pharaoh do to me? He'll feed me to the desert jackals!"

PYR-A-MIDION'S SECRET

We followed the voice and found a mouse with a shaved head crying **_desperately_**.

"Ahem! Can we help you?" Professor von Volt asked.

The mouse dried a tear on his **elegant** pleated linen tunic and shook his head. The turquoise necklace he wore **_jingled_** as he spoke.

Pyr-a-midion

"I'm afraid no mouse can help me," he said with a ꕷꕷꕷ sigh.

"My name is **Pyr-a-midion**." He blew his nose loudly on a palm leaf.

BPRRRRRRRRR!

"Until a week ago, I was the pharaoh's **GRanD VizieR**, and my name was respected all over Egypt. I can still hear the people chanting: Pyr-a-midion! Pyr-a-midion! Pyr-a-midion! In other words, I was **famouse**. But then . . ."

"But then what?" we all asked together.

Trap sat down in the sand and propped his feet up on a rock.

"I'm gonna make myself comfortable," he grumbled. "Looks like this is going to be a **loooooooong story**!"

"As I was saying," Pyr-a-midion continued, "a week ago, that **SNeaKy**, no-good rodent came to court. In other words — Mousehotep!"

"Mousehotep?!" we all shouted together.

"Yes, yes, Mousehotep," he replied. "He's the one. He's truly, truly **WICKED**! That rascal started to plot against me. And then . . ."

"And then what?" we all asked together.

"And then one week ago, my wife, Pyr-a-midina, made some almond cookies for the pharaoh. 'Be sure they're really, really GOOD!' I warned her. 'I'll put in loads of ALMONDS!' she assured me. And she did. But alas, a TINY fragment of almond shell ended up in one of the cookies. When Ramesses bit into the cookie, he chipped his front tooth! And then . . ."

"And then what?" we all yelled together.

Pyr-a-midion pulled at his whiskers in **DESPERATION**.

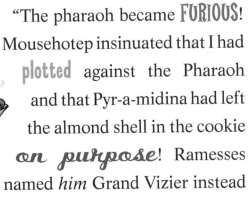

Pyr-a-midina

"The pharaoh became FURIOUS! Mousehotep insinuated that I had plotted against the Pharaoh and that Pyr-a-midina had left the almond shell in the cookie *on purpose*! Ramesses named *him* Grand Vizier instead of me. The pharaoh was about to feed me to the crocodiles for dinner when . . ."

"When what?" we all shouted together.

"I knew this was going to be a **LOOOOONG** story," Trap mumbled.

"My wife threw herself at Nefertari's feet and asked for MERCY," Pyr-a-midion continued. "The queen was moved, and I was given one last chance. But then . . ."

"But then what?" we all yelled together again.

"Then the **MALICIOUS** Mousehotep suggested the pharaoh give me an extremely **DIFFICULT** puzzle to solve to gain my freedom. The pharaoh gave me seven days to solve it, and my time is up right **now**. When the sun rises, I'll be breakfast for crocodiles!"

The soldiers that were snoozing in the melon field behind the oasis **yawned**. They were about to take Pyr-a-midion away!

The prisoner cast a nervous glance at them and shuddered.

"What's the puzzle?" Benjamin asked sweetly. "Maybe we can **help** you solve it."

Pyr-a-midion sighed.

"It's **VERY**, **VERY**, **VERY** difficult," he explained. "In fact, it's impossible to solve. It's the Riddle of the Sphinx! No mouse has been able to solve it, **ever**!"

THE RIDDLE OF THE SPHINX

THE RIDDLE OF THE SPHINX

WHAT ANIMAL WALKS ON FOUR FEET
WHEN HE'S YOUNG, ON TWO FEET
WHEN HE'S AN ADULT, AND ON THREE
FEET WHEN HE'S OLD?

Pyr-a-midion read the puzzle aloud to us. Then he blew his nose loudly on a palm leaf.

Bprrrrrrrrr!

"I've thought about it for seven **days** and seven NIGHTS, but I haven't come up with the answer," he sobbed. "What animal first has four feet, then two, and finally three? Oh, may the **SCARABS** save me!"

Professor von Volt closed his eyes and concentrated. Suddenly, he opened his eyes.

"Aha!" he shouted. "I've got it! It's us! When we're babies, we crawl, which is **FOUR** feet, when we're adults, we walk on **TWO**, and when we're old, we lean on a cane, so that becomes **THREE** feet!"

Pyr-a-midion hugged the professor with glee.

"Oh, thank you!" he told him. "Now I can go back and give Mousehotep the **CORRECT** answer!"

"I'm going to do you a favor, my friend," Trap said with a chuckle. "I'm going to tell you some *clever* questions you can ask Mousehotep. I guarantee he won't be able to answer them! He'll look bad, and the pharaoh will ask you to be the **Grand Vizier** again."

CLEVER QUESTIONS FOR MOUSEHOTEP

1. A brick weighs one pound plus a half a brick. How much does a brick weigh?

2. If you have ten sarcophagi, and I take all but three, how many sarcophagi are left?

3. Crocodile eggs are hatching in the swamp. The number of crocodiles doubles every minute. After one hour, the swamp is full of crocodiles. After how many minutes was it half full?

4. A sailor is painting a ship on the dock in Memphis. He is standing on a nine-and-a-half-foot ladder. The rungs are eight inches apart. The sailor is standing on the lowest rung, which is twelve inches from the surface of the water. The dock's tide rises three feet every hour. How many rungs does the sailor have to climb to stay dry?

5. A pharaoh has to take a cat, a mouse, and a piece of cheese to Thebes. To get to Thebes, he has to cross the Nile on a boat. There's only room on the boat for the pharaoh and one of the three. If the pharaoh leaves the cat alone with the mouse, or the mouse alone with the cheese, one will eat the other. What should the pharaoh do?

6. The sum of the pharaoh's age, the Grand Vizier's age, and the chief guard's age is eighty-four. In ten years, what will the sum of their ages be?

7. If a choir of twenty mice takes three minutes to sing a song, how many minutes will a choir of ten mice take to sing the same song?

 Which of the two figures has a bigger area: the black circle or the black ring?

Which of the two horizontal lines is longer?

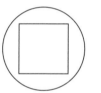

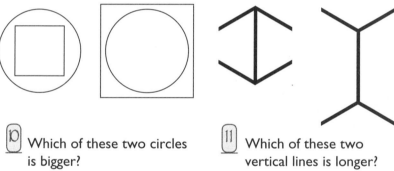

Which of these two circles is bigger?

Which of these two vertical lines is longer?

CLEVER ANSWERS

1. Two pounds. 2. Three are left. 3. After 59 minutes. 4. The number of steps out of the water remains the same because the ship goes up with the tide. 5. The pharaoh should take the mouse to Thebes by boat and return empty-handed. He should then take the cat to Thebes and return with the mouse. Then he should take the cheese to Thebes, leave it safely with the cat, and return empty-handed. Finally, he should take the mouse to Thebes. 6. 114 (84+30). 7. Three minutes. 8. The ring has a larger area than the circle. 9. They are the same length. 10. They are the same size. 11. They are the same length.

THE SECRET OF THE GREAT PYRAMID

Pyr-a-midion hugged us.

"Thank you all **SO** much!" he said. "How can I ever make it up to you? Ask for anything you want."

The professor put a paw on his shoulder.

"Dear Pyr-a-midion, it was our pleasure to help you," he said.

"Hey, Professor," Trap whispered. "Ask him how the **pyramids** are built!"

"Ahem, there is something," the professor said. "As a scholar, I would like to know how the pyramids are built."

"That is a **very** interesting question!" Pyr-a-midion replied with a chuckle.

Thea surreptitiously snapped a splendid **PHOTO**

with the Sphinx in the background as Professor
von Volt began taking notes.

EGYPT

THE GREAT SPHINX OF GIZA

This famous statue has the body of a
lion and the head of a man. It is 241
feet long, 66 feet high, and 63 feet
wide, and was carved from a single
piece of limestone. Experts believe
the Sphinx was originally painted in
bright colors.

Professor von Volt's Notes

Egyptologists believe the Great Pyramid of Giza was built as a tomb for the pharaoh Khufu (Cheops in Greek), around 2560 BC. The pyramid was originally 481 feet tall, but today it is just 455 feet tall, as the tip has eroded over time. There are two smaller pyramids near the Great Pyramid of Giza — one built as a tomb for the pharaoh Khafre, and another built as a tomb for the pharaoh Menkaure.

More than 2,300,000 stone blocks were used, and each block weighed around 2.5 tons.

It took at least twenty years to build the Great Pyramid.

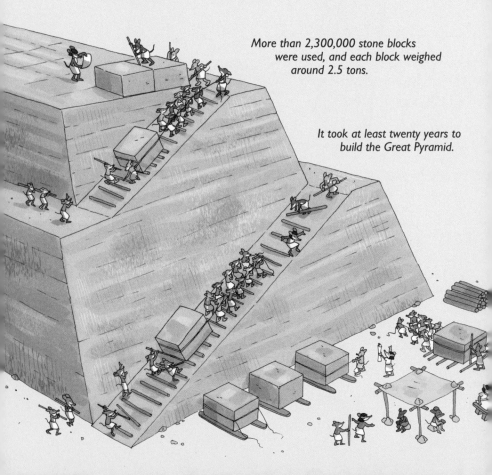

It took at least 20,000–30,000 workers to build the Great Pyramid. These workers were not slaves; they were willing workers who often traveled from faraway villages. It was an honor to be part of the construction crew!

In the interior of the pyramid, there are both ascending and descending passageways as well as two rooms, the king's and the queen's chambers.

The pyramid was covered with a layer of white limestone that made the structure highly reflective in the light of the sun.

Many of the blocks that make up the pyramid are made of limestone, while other blocks are made of granite. It is generally believed that the Egyptians used copper or stone saws, chisels, and drills.

No one is entirely certain exactly how the Great Pyramid was constructed. Many believe workers pulled the stones up a series of ramps using special sleds. The workers most likely raised the large individual stone blocks into position using wooden and bronze levers.

ON THE ROAD AGAIN!

We thanked Pyr-a-midion for revealing the ancient secrets of the pyramids. Then we said good-bye to him and Bab-beot and hurried back to our time machine. We had seen the only remaining wonder of the **Seven Wonders of the Ancient World**, and our visit to ancient Egypt had been a success.

Oh, how I wished I could head home to my cozy mouse hole in New Mouse City! But instead we were heading to medieval England to visit the court of the legendary King Arthur. We all climbed into the **MOUSE MOVER 3000** and Professor von Volt **SET** the Chronometer.

BANGGGGGGGGGGGGGGGGG!!!

My paws gripped the arms of the chair, and my head spun like a top.

The time machine began to vibrate, spinning faster and faster!

The little ship filled with a mysterious BLUE fog.

I wondered what **incredible** adventures awaited us in medieval England. Would I witness a joust between two knights? Or explore a medieval castle? Who knows? I promise I'll tell you all about it in my next book — **mouse's honor**.

So farewell until then, dear mouse friends!

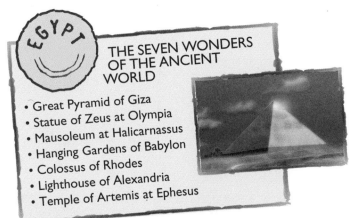

EGYPT

THE SEVEN WONDERS OF THE ANCIENT WORLD

- Great Pyramid of Giza
- Statue of Zeus at Olympia
- Mausoleum at Halicarnassus
- Hanging Gardens of Babylon
- Colossus of Rhodes
- Lighthouse of Alexandria
- Temple of Artemis at Ephesus

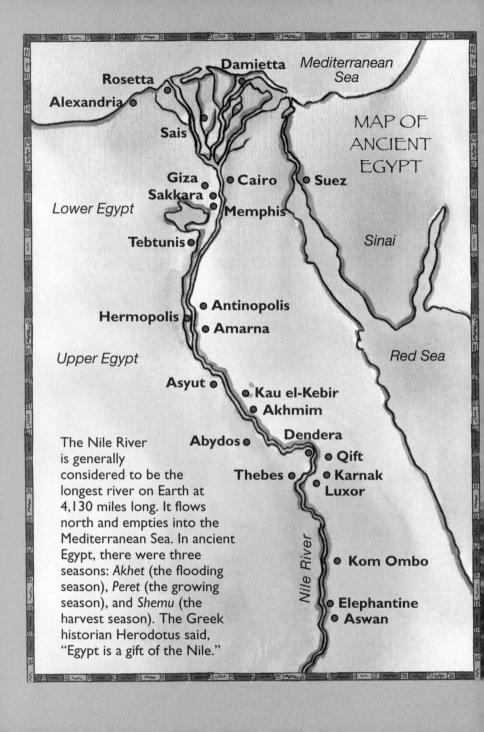

Damietta

Rosetta

Alexandria

Mediterranean
Sea

Sais

MAP OF
ANCIENT
EGYPT

Giza
Sakkara

Cairo

Suez

Lower Egypt

Memphis

Tebtunis

Sinai

Antinopolis

Hermopolis

Amarna

Upper Egypt

Red Sea

Asyut

Kau el-Kebir

Akhmim

Abydos

Dendera

Thebes

Qift

Karnak

Luxor

The Nile River
is generally
considered to be the
longest river on Earth at
4,130 miles long. It flows
north and empties into the
Mediterranean Sea. In ancient
Egypt, there were three
seasons: *Akhet* (the flooding
season), *Peret* (the growing
season), and *Shemu* (the
harvest season). The Greek
historian Herodotus said,
"Egypt is a gift of the Nile."

Nile River

Kom Ombo

Elephantine

Aswan

Dear rodent friends,

I hope you have enjoyed reading all about my adventures during my journey through ancient Egypt. To keep the memories from fading, I wrote this very special **travel journal** just for you. It's full of **definitions**, **MAPS**, and **FUN FACTS**.

Learn about the Egyptian calendar, the secrets of pyramid construction, and how to make your very own ancient Egyptian bracelet. You'll find it's like taking off again on a fabumouse journey through time!

Geronimo Stilton

FUN FACTS

The oldest pyramid . . .
is the Pyramid of Djoser in the Sahara Desert in Egypt, northwest of the city of Memphis. It was built during the 27th century B.C. for the Pharaoh Djoser and was originally 203 feet tall.

The oldest obelisk . . .
is that of Senusret in Heliopolis. It is 67 feet tall, weighs 120 tons (240,000 pounds), and is made of red granite.

The tallest obelisk . . .
is that of Tuthmosis III. Today it stands in the Piazza San Giovanni in Laterano, Rome, where it has been since 1588. It is 105 feet tall.

The oldest hieroglyphs . . .
come from Abydos, 300 miles south of Cairo. The symbols were found on pieces of pottery, bone and ivory tags, and clay seal impressions that are dated between 3400 and 3200 BC.

Help the Egyptian architect take the pyramid's measurements by telling him how many triangles make up this pyramid.

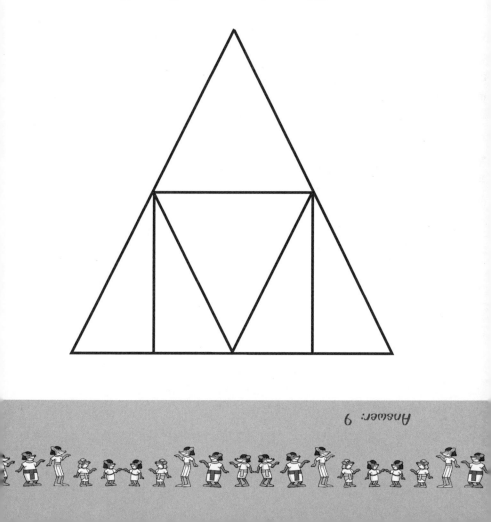

EGYPT
MINI DICTIONARY

amulet: A charm or object that is said to have magical powers that protect the owner.

archaeology: The study of the distant past, which often involves digging up old buildings, objects, and bones and examining them carefully.

cubit: An ancient form of measurement based on the length of the forearm, measured from the elbow to the tip of the middle finger. Usually equal to about 18-20 inches (46-52 centimeters).

deben: Ancient Egyptian stone used as a measurement for weight. Copper deben weighed about 13.6 grams each, while gold deben weighed about 23.7 grams each. Deben could be used as currency in exchange for goods and services.

Egyptology: The study of the civilization of ancient Egypt.

hieroglyphics: A system of writing used by ancient Egyptians, made up of pictures and symbols that stand for words.

mastaba: An Egyptian tomb that is oblong-shaped with sloping sides and a flat roof, like the base of a pyramid.

necropolis: Place dedicated to burials and worship of the dead.

obelisk: An upright 4-sided pillar built out of one piece of stone that gradually tapers as it rises and ends in a pyramid on top. It was usually decorated with inscriptions.

papyrus: A tall water plant that grows in northern Africa and southern Europe. Ancient Egyptians used the stems of the plant to make writing paper.

pyramid: An ancient Egyptian stone monument where pharaohs and their treasures were buried.

WRITE, SCRIBE!

1. Imagine you're an inventor. How would you design traps and pitfalls to prevent thieves from entering the tomb of the great pharaoh? Write your ideas down on a separate sheet of paper, and include some drawings.

Thieves will never be able to get in!

2. Imagine you're an archeologist entering the funereal chamber of the pharaoh. What objects do you find in the chamber? Write about them on a separate sheet of paper.

3. Queen Nefertari decided to have a birthday party for Ramesses the Great. The throne hall was decorated for the occasion, and musicians and dancers were entertaining the guests. What do you think happened at the party? Write about it on a separate sheet of paper.

The crane, forklift, computer, jackhammer, truck, and cement mixer are not from ancient Egypt.

what's wrong with this picture?

There are six objects in this drawing that are not from ancient Egypt. Can you spot them?

Egyptian Calendar

The Egyptian year was made up of 365 days and had three seasons made up of four months each:

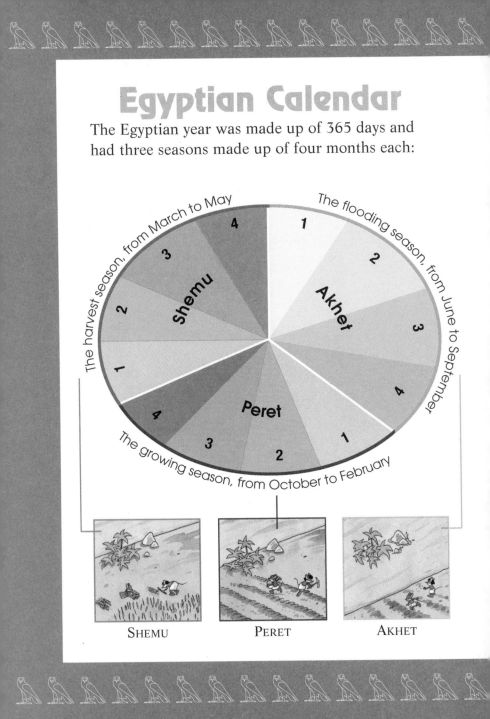

The flooding season, from June to September

The harvest season, from March to May

The growing season, from October to February

Akhet

Shemu

Peret

SHEMU

PERET

AKHET

Every month was made up of thirty days, divided into three weeks of ten days each.

New Year's Day fell in mid-July, which is when the waters of the Nile River began to rise rapidly. It was preceded by five days of great festivities to honor of the birth of:

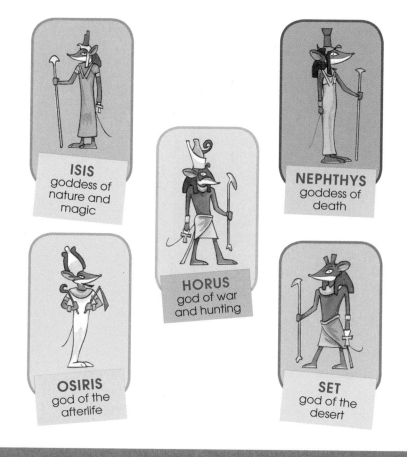

ISIS
goddess of nature and magic

NEPHTHYS
goddess of death

HORUS
god of war and hunting

OSIRIS
god of the afterlife

SET
god of the desert

WHY DID EGYPTIANS DRAW FIGURES IN PROFILE?

A profile of a head makes the features more recognizable. The position of the feet and arms when shown in profile show the direction the figure was walking.

Notice that in the profiles shown above, the figures' eyes and torsos are turned toward the viewer, showing off their clothing and jewelry.

MUMMY FINGER

Convince your friends you've found a mummy's finger in your backyard!

1. Cut a hole the size of your index finger in the bottom of a shoe box.

2. Hide the hole by filling the box with cotton balls, cut-up strips of newspaper, or packing peanuts.

3. Wrap your index finger with bandages and put it through the hole.

4. Place the cover on the box and tell your friends you found a mummy's finger. Then remove the cover and show the "mummified" finger. If you really want to scare your friends, move your finger suddenly. They'll think the finger has come alive!

WRITE, SCRIBE!

1. In ancient Egypt, the fertile bank of the Nile River was the ideal place for growing crops. Imagine you're a farmer in Egypt. Write about your family and describe everyone's duties on a separate sheet of paper.

2. What do you like best about ancient Egypt? Write your thoughts on a separate sheet of paper.

Everyone has a job on the farm.

TO THE ANCIENT EGYPTIANS, EVERY COLOR HAD A PARTICULAR SIGNIFICANCE:

GREEN represented regeneration, youth, and new life.

TURQUOISE symbolized joy and the color of sunrise, and was considered the color of promise and the future.

RED was the color of chaos, disorder, and the desert. It represented fire, fury, destruction, and danger.

BLACK was the color of earth fertilized by the flooding waters of the Nile. Therefore, it represented rebirth, fertility, new life, and resurrection.

YELLOW was the color of gold, the sun, and the skin of the gods. It could also represent perfection.

WHITE symbolized purity, simplicity, and cleanliness.

BLUE represented water and the color of the floods and the heavens.

EGYPTIAN BRACELETS

In ancient Egypt, both males and females wore bracelets decorated with engravings and amulets. Try making one!

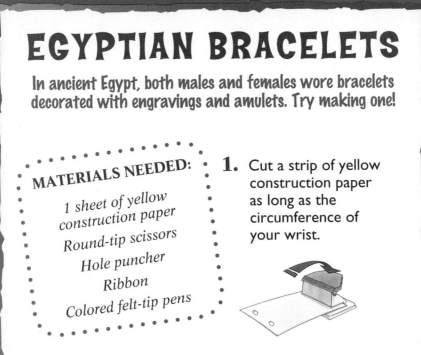

MATERIALS NEEDED:

1 sheet of yellow construction paper

Round-tip scissors

Hole puncher

Ribbon

Colored felt-tip pens

1. Cut a strip of yellow construction paper as long as the circumference of your wrist.

2. Punch two holes on either end of the strip of paper.

3. Use your felt-tip pens to decorate the bracelet by drawing Egyptian symbols, designs, geometric, shapes, and figures.

4. Place the bracelet on your wrist, slip the ribbon through the holes, and tie it in a knot.

ENJOY WEARING YOUR BRACELET!

You might even want to try making one for a friend.

GAMES IN ANCIENT EGYPT

PUZZLES

A puzzle is an image that has been cut up into many small pieces. The fragments need to be put back together to reveal the original design. In ancient Egypt, puzzle pieces were made of wood and animal bones.

WOODEN TOYS

Egyptian children played with toys that were carved from wood. Popular toys included spinning tops, crocodiles, cats, and boats. Some wooden toys had wheels and ropes so that children could pull the toys behind them.

OBSTACLE COURSES

Children would design a course with obstacles such as a cross bar or a small ditch that had to be jumped over. They would then take turns completing the course and competing to see who could finish fastest.

Check out all of my journeys through time!

#1: DINOSAUR DISASTER

#2: PYRAMID PUZZLE

#3: MEDIEVAL MISSION

Don't miss any of my other fabumouse adventures!

#1 Lost Treasure of the Emerald Eye

#2 The Curse of the Cheese Pyramid

#3 Cat and Mouse in a Haunted House

#4 I'm Too Fond of My Fur!

#5 Four Mice Deep in the Jungle

#6 Paws Off, Cheddarface!

#7 Red Pizzas for a Blue Count

#8 Attack of the Bandit Cats

#9 A Fabumouse Vacation for Geronimo

#10 All Because of a Cup of Coffee

#11 It's Halloween, You 'Fraidy Mouse!

#12 Merry Christmas, Geronimo!

#13 The Phantom of the Subway

#14 The Temple of the Ruby of Fire

#15 The Mona Mousa Code

#16 A Cheese-Colored Camper

#17 Watch Your Whiskers, Stilton!

#18 Shipwreck on the Pirate Islands

#19 My Name Is Stilton, Geronimo Stilton

#20 Surf's Up, Geronimo!

#21 The Wild, Wild West

#22 The Secret of Cacklefur Castle

A Christmas Tale

#23 Valentine's Day Disaster

#24 Field Trip to Niagara Falls

#25 The Search for Sunken Treasure

#26 The Mummy with No Name

#27 The Christmas Toy Factory

#28 Wedding Crasher

#29 Down and Out Down Under

#30 The Mouse Island Marathon

#31 The Mysterious Cheese Thief

Christmas Catastrophe

#32 Valley of the Giant Skeletons

#33 Geronimo and the Gold Medal Mystery

#34 Geronimo Stilton, Secret Agent

#35 A Very Merry Christmas

#36 Geronimo's Valentine

#37 The Race Across America

#38 A Fabumouse School Adventure

#39 Singing Sensation

#40 The Karate Mouse

#41 Mighty Mount Kilimanjaro

#42 The Peculiar Pumpkin Thief

#43 I'm Not a Supermouse!

#44 The Giant Diamond Robbery

#45 Save the White Whale!

#46 The Haunted Castle

#47 Run for the Hills, Geronimo!

#48 The Mystery in Venice

#49 The Way of the Samurai

#50 This Hotel Is Haunted

#51 The Enormouse Pearl Heist

#52 Mouse in Space!

#53 Rumble in the Jungle

#54 Get into Gear, Stilton!

#55 The Golden Statue Plot

#56 Flight of the Red Bandit

The Hunt for the Golden Book

Special Edition!

Meet
GERONIMO STILTONOOT

He is a cavemouse — Geronimo Stilton's ancient ancestor! He runs the stone newspaper in the prehistoric village of Old Mouse City. From dealing with dinosaurs to dodging meteorites, his life in the Stone Age is full of adventure!

#1 The Stone of Fire

#2 Watch Your Tail!

#3 Help, I'm in Hot Lava!

#4 The Fast and the Frozen